We're Riding on a Caravan

An Adventure on the Silk Road

To Dee and Don, with love — L. K.

For Charlotte Welply — keep traveling, with much love — H. C.

Barefoot Books
2067 Massachusetts Ave
Cambridge, MA 02140

This book was typeset in Caslon
The illustrations were prepared in watercolor, graphite and collage on 140lb Bockingford paper

Graphic design by Louise Millar, London
Color separation by Grafiscan
Printed and bound in China

This book has been printed on 100% acid-free paper

Library of Congress Cataloging-in-Publication Data

Krebs, Laurie.
We're riding on a caravan / written by Laurie Krebs ; illustrated by Helen Cann.
 p. cm.
Summary: Rhyming text introduces the sights and sounds of the Silk Road, such as the Yellow River, the oasis at Dunhuang, the rugged desert
near Hami, and the excitement of the market at Kashgar. Includes a history of this trade route and the places where people stopped along the way.
ISBN 1-84148-343-5 (hardcover : alk. paper) 1. China, Northwest--Description and travel--Juvenile literature. 2. Silk Road--Description
and travel--Juvenile literature. I. Cann, Helen, 1969- ill. II. Title.
DS793.N6K74 2005
950--dc22

2004028591

3 5 7 9 8 6 4 2

We're Riding on a Caravan

An Adventure on the Silk Road

Written by Laurie Krebs

Illustrated by Helen Cann

Barefoot Books
Celebrating Art and Story

We're riding on a caravan, a bumpy, humpy caravan,

We're riding on a caravan to places far away.

A year ago we left Xi'an, the summer sun was bright.
We tugged our camels to their feet and tied the cargo tight.
We passed beneath the city gate and heard the Tower Bell.
Before we took the Silk Road west, we stopped to wave farewell.

We're riding on a caravan, a bumpy, humpy caravan,

We're riding on a caravan to places far away.

Nine months ago we reached Lanzhou, as leaves began to fall.
We crossed the Yellow River and drew near the city wall.
We traded silk for bags of wool. We liked its pleasant smell.
We bought fresh fruit and vegetables to eat and take to sell.

We're riding on a caravan, a bumpy, humpy caravan,

We're riding on a caravan to places far away.

Six months ago we reached Dunhuang. A brisk wind chilled the air.
Around the lush oasis, there were sand dunes everywhere.
We sold some silk and precious stones. We traded rice for bread.
We filled our jugs with water for the desert road ahead.

We're riding on a caravan, a bumpy, humpy caravan,

We're riding on a caravan to places far away.

Five months ago we reached Hami, worn out and sick and cold.
For winter in the desert was as harsh as we'd been told.
We warmed ourselves with goat-head soup and steaming cups of tea,
And rested there for several days before we left Hami.

We're riding on a caravan, a bumpy, humpy caravan,

We're riding on a caravan to places far away.

Three months ago we reached Turpan and felt the touch of spring.
We passed fresh fields and vineyards that were just awakening.
We stopped to trade at mud-brick huts where grapes were hung to dry,
To turn into the raisins that the caravans would buy.

We're riding on a caravan, a bumpy, humpy caravan,

We're riding on a caravan to places far away.

A week ago, we reached Kashgar. Our journey's end was near,

For it was summer once again and we'd been gone a year.

Our bodies were exhausted and the camels' feet were sore.

The trip along the Silk Road was two thousand miles or more!

We're stopping with our caravan, our bumpy, humpy caravan

We're stopping with our caravan and for a while we'll stay.

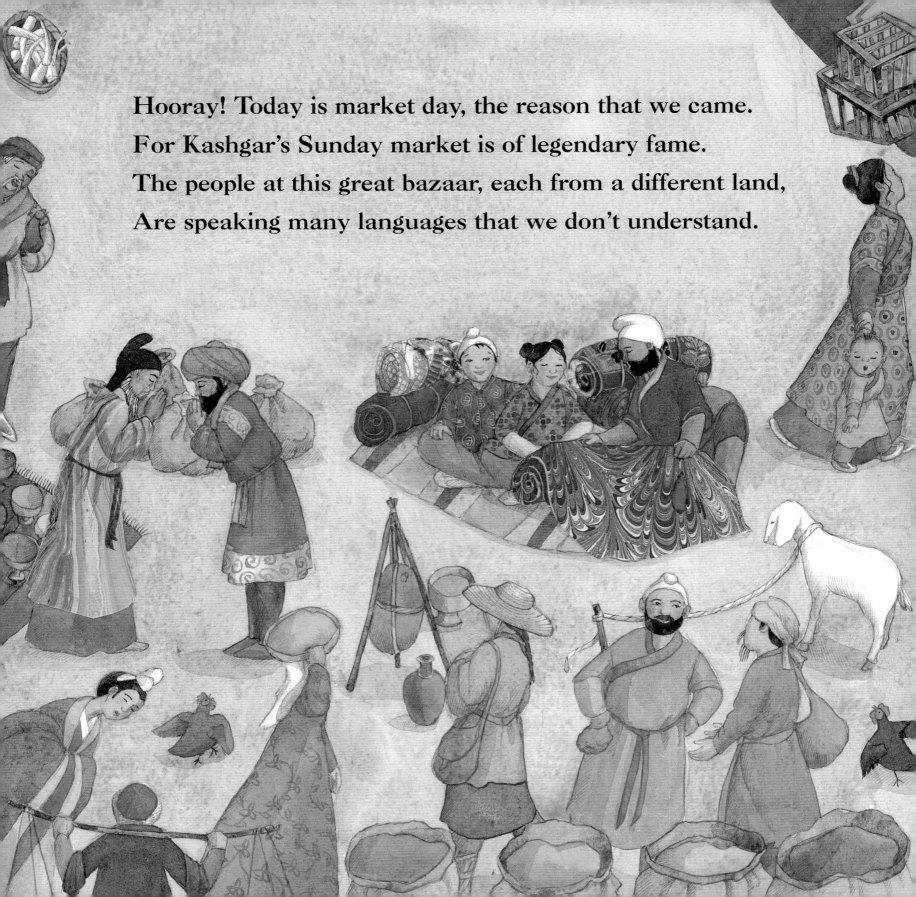

Hooray! Today is market day, the reason that we came.

For Kashgar's Sunday market is of legendary fame.

The people at this great bazaar, each from a different land,

Are speaking many languages that we don't understand.

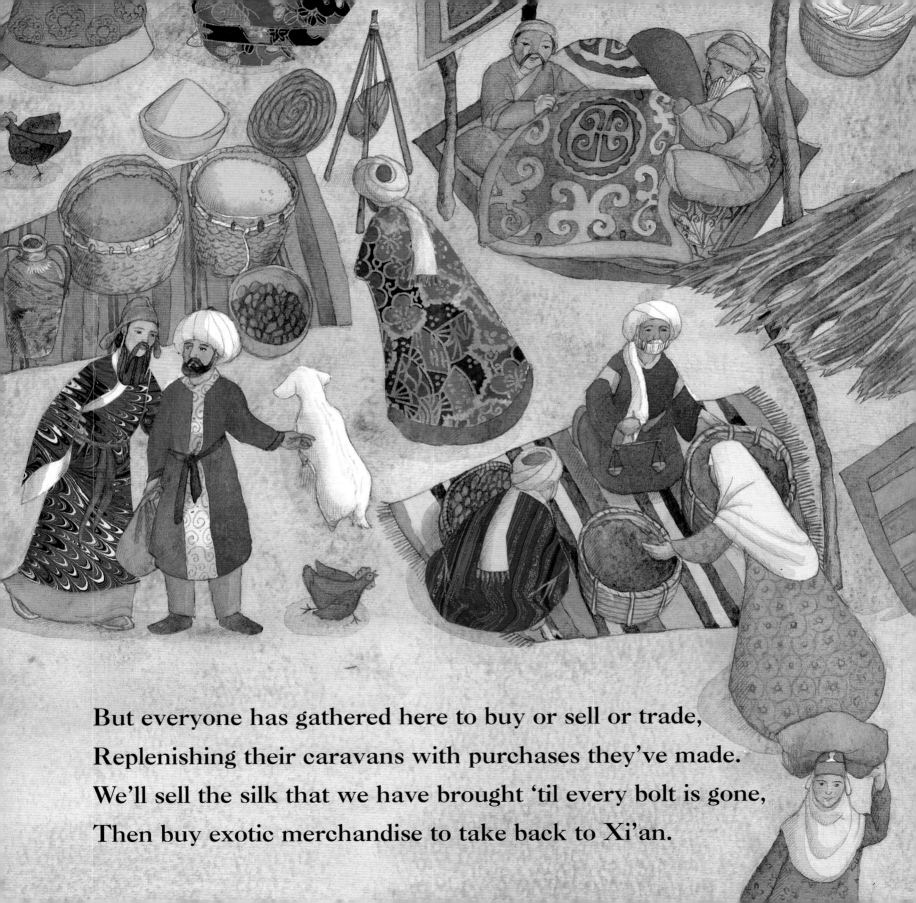

But everyone has gathered here to buy or sell or trade,
Replenishing their caravans with purchases they've made.
We'll sell the silk that we have brought 'til every bolt is gone,
Then buy exotic merchandise to take back to Xi'an.

There's ivory from India and curry spice and teas,
And carpets from the Middle East and woven tapestries.
And horses from Arabia and flocks of goats and sheep,
And hairy yaks from mountain towns, where snow and ice pile deep.

We're loading up our caravan, our bumpy, humpy caravan

Too soon the sun is setting and the market shutters down.
The caravans are piled high, preparing to leave town.
For some will make the journey through the mountains to the west,
And some will take the southern route because they know it best.

We're loading up our caravan, for home is far away.

But we will travel to the east. We've done it all before.
We'll travel on the Silk Road 'til we reach Xi'an once more.

MONGOLIA

Gobi Desert

South China Sea

The Great Wall of China

Sunwei Mountains

LANZHOU

Xi'an

The Yellow River

CHINA

The Story of Silk

It all began with a young Chinese empress, a little worm and a big secret...

In ancient times, so the story goes, the Chinese emperor's new bride, Hsi Ling-shi, was sitting in her garden beneath a mulberry tree. A cocoon fell from above into her cup of hot tea; and as she drew it from the water, it unraveled into a long, delicate thread of silk.

From this accident, the Chinese discovered how to form thread from the cocoons of silkworm moths. Hundreds of tiny worms (actually caterpillars) hatched from the moths' eggs. For six weeks they feasted night and day on mulberry leaves until they were large enough to spin cocoons.

The cocoons were gathered by workers, who softened them with steam or hot air. Unwinding several cocoons at a time, they carefully twisted the hairlike strands into silk thread. Then the thread was woven into cloth and dyed in a rich palette of colors.

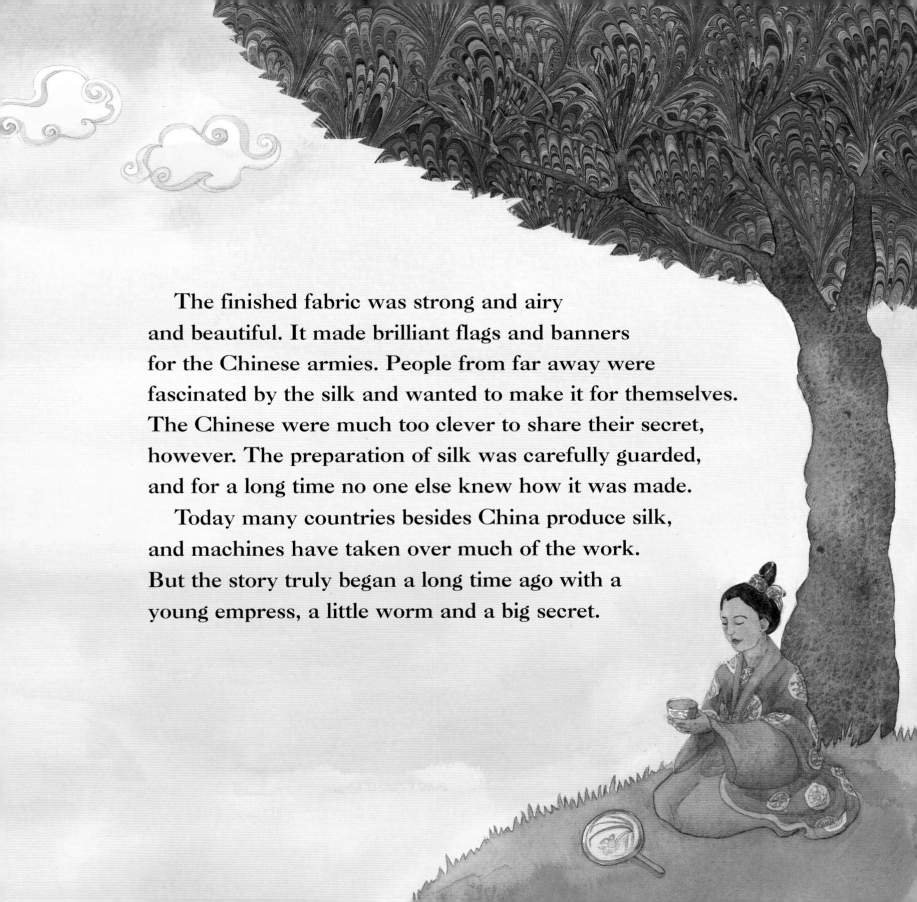

The finished fabric was strong and airy
and beautiful. It made brilliant flags and banners
for the Chinese armies. People from far away were
fascinated by the silk and wanted to make it for themselves.
The Chinese were much too clever to share their secret,
however. The preparation of silk was carefully guarded,
and for a long time no one else knew how it was made.

Today many countries besides China produce silk,
and machines have taken over much of the work.
But the story truly began a long time ago with a
young empress, a little worm and a big secret.

The History of the Silk Road

The caravan path known as the Silk Road is thousands of years old. Historians think the long, long path was the first trade route between the peoples of Europe and the Orient.

Europeans loved Chinese silk and were eager to buy it. So caravans, laden with fabric, traveled west through mountain kingdoms and desert villages to deliver it. But silk was not their only cargo. The Chinese also carried furs, spices, metals, jade, ceramics and lacquerware. On their way, they stopped at oases and trading posts to sell their goods, barter for new things and buy water and supplies. At the same time, caravans traveling east from Europe brought gems, gold, silver, ivory, tapestries and perfume to the Orient.

Very few caravans made the entire trip along the Silk Road. It was much too long! Usually caravans would stop at a place where people could rest. New drivers and fresh animals would continue the journey. Often the people returned home, but sometimes they stayed to raise their families in the new village. This way, different groups of people came to live along the Silk Road. They brought with them new religions and art, new languages and inventions and, best of all, new ideas.

China's Silk Road is only part of the ancient caravan path. One route continued west from Kashgar through the mountains to Samarkand and Central Asia. Another followed a southern route through mountain passes into India. The Silk Road even reached all the way to Europe! Today many of the Chinese oases mentioned in this story are bustling cities, just as they must have been centuries ago.

One of the most famous explorers who passed along the Silk Road was Marco Polo. Almost eight hundred years ago, he traveled between Italy and China, a journey that took several years. We are lucky to have his stories that tell us about the people he met and the things he saw as he made his way along the ancient Silk Road.

Places Along the Chinese Silk Road

Xi'an (shee-*ahn*)

The ancient city of Xi'an was the starting point for caravans heading west along the Silk Road. Located in the fertile valleys of the Wei and Yellow Rivers, Xi'an's old city walls and gates, pagodas and bell towers still exist amidst the city's modern buildings. The famous Terracotta Warriors, said to have guarded the tomb of an early emperor (221–210 BC), were uncovered in 1974, making Xi'an a popular tourist and archaeological site today.

Lanzhou (lahn-*joe*)

Lanzhou, the capital of Ganzu province, was an important caravan stop along the Silk Road. More than three hundred miles west of Xi'an and nestled in a narrow valley between barren hills, Lanzhou's mild climate and location along the Yellow River made it a useful link between Tibet, Mongolia and other parts of China. Goods were shipped along the river on rafts of inflated animal hide, and with the cargo came new people, who settled among the Han Chinese.

Dunhuang (dun-*wang*)

Six hundred miles from Lanzhou, at the end of China's Great Wall, lay another principal trading post, Dunhuang. Caravan drivers from both the east and west stopped to replenish their supplies and give thanks for safe passage through the dangerous country. The Mogao Caves, which house a treasure trove of Buddhist manuscripts, wall paintings and sculpture, reflect the travelers' gratitude as well as their hopes for continued safety.

Hami (hah-*mee*)

Hami, set below sea level, two hundred miles from Dunhuang, was the next major stop on the Silk Road. Its diverse population includes a number of minority groups such as the Hui, Kazakhs, Mongols and Uygurs in addition to the Han Chinese. Hami is famous for its sweet melons, which were a favorite item of trade for the caravans. The oasis borders the Taklamakan Desert, which means "go in and never come out" and which was a hazard for travelers on the Silk Road.

Turpan (tuhr-*pan*)

Two hundred miles past Hami was the oasis of Turpan, another significant caravan stop. Like Hami, it rests below sea level, experiences extreme temperature changes and is dominated by the Taklamakan Desert. However, karez channels, an underground water system fed by streams from the Flaming Mountains, irrigate lush fields and vineyards. White raisins, the area's most famous crop, have been dried in open mud-brick buildings and sold in markets for centuries.

Kashgar (kash-*gahr*)

The fabled city of Kashgar was the last oasis on China's Silk Road, nearly seven hundred and fifty miles from Turpan and close to the country's western border. Here, at the foot of the Pamir Mountains, at the juncture of China's northern and southern caravan routes, weary travelers found rest and fresh supplies. Kashgar's Sunday market, still in existence, remains a melting pot of cultures and languages, religions and traditions, reflecting the varied faces of China.

Barefoot Books
Celebrating Art and Story

At Barefoot Books, we celebrate art and story with books that open
the hearts and minds of children from all walks of life, inspiring them to read
deeper, search further, and explore their own creative gifts. Taking our
inspiration from many different cultures, we focus on themes that encourage
independence of spirit, enthusiasm for learning, and acceptance of other
traditions. Thoughtfully prepared by writers, artists and storytellers from
all over the world, our products combine the best of the present with the best
of the past to educate our children as the caretakers of tomorrow.

www.barefootbooks.com